ZENOBIA AND MOUSE

Written by
VIVIAN FRENCH

Illustrated by
DUNCAN SMITH

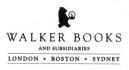

WALKER BOOKS
AND SUBSIDIARIES
LONDON • BOSTON • SYDNEY

For Jimie, Gus, Lucy, Nancy and Molly,
who always said, "Story please!"

First published 1990 by Walker Books Ltd
87 Vauxhall Walk, London SE11 5HJ

This edition published 1997

2 4 6 8 10 9 7 5 3

Text © 1990 Vivian French
Illustrations © 1990 Duncan Smith

This book has been typeset in Plantin.

Printed and bound in Great Britain by
The Guernsey Press Co. Ltd

British Library Cataloguing in Publication Data
A catalogue record for this book is
available from the British Library.

ISBN 0-7445-5451-9

"Duncan Smith's exquisite pencil drawings reveal that Zenobia has a Black Dad and a White Mum – and a toy mouse of enormouse character – in an engaging collection of stories by Vivian French." *The Guardian*

Vivian French became a broadcast poet on *Children's Hour* at the tender age of six. Some years later, she worked in children's theatre, both as an actor and a writer, and is now an author and storyteller. She has written many children's books, including *Mary Poggs and the Sunshine* and three collections of original fairytales, *Under the Moon, The Thistle Princess* and *The Boy Who Walked on Water*. She is also the author of *A Song for Little Toad* (shortlisted for the 1995 Smarties Book Prize); *Lazy Jack*; *Please, Princess Primrose* and several other picture books, as well as the Read and Wonder non-fiction titles *Caterpillar Caterpillar* (shortlisted for the 1993 Kurt Maschler Award); *The Apple Trees* and *Spider Watching*. She has four daughters, two cats and a guinea-pig and lives in Bristol.

Duncan Smith is the illustrator of the Walker books *Jake's Magic* and *Just Bear and Friends*.

"Oh, Mouse . . . dear Mouse, did you hear me?"
"I'm not deaf," Mouse said.

CONTENTS

*Dollie May was leaning against the sugar bowl,
smiling her blue-eyed happy smile.*

DOLLIE
MAY

Zenobia finished her mouthful of cornflakes and put down her spoon.

"I had a dream last night," she said. "Shall I tell you?"

No one answered. Zenobia made a face at Dollie May and picked up her spoon again. Dollie May was leaning against the sugar bowl, smiling her blue-eyed happy smile.

"It was a very NOISY dream," said Zenobia, in a cornflaky voice. Dollie May went on smiling.

Mum turned round from the sink. "Don't talk with your mouth full, lovey," she said. "And could you hurry up a little? Annie will be here soon."

"P'raps Annie will want to hear about my dream," Zenobia said. "No one else does." She offered Dollie May the last spoonful of her breakfast, and Dollie May slipped sideways off the table. Zenobia was just in time to stop the sugar bowl slipping after her, but some of the sugar went too quickly to catch.

"Oh, Zenobia!" Mum said. "*Please* don't make a mess — I've got ever such a busy morning."

"It was Dollie May who did it," Zenobia said. "I caught the bowl."

"Well," said Mum, getting out the dustpan and brush, "why don't you go and look out of the window? You can tell me when Annie arrives — her dad's bringing some bits and pieces for the school jumble sale."

"Can I tell you about my dream first?" Zenobia asked.

"Just let me sweep up the sugar and clear

the table," Mum said, piling up plates and bowls and cereal packets. "Then you can tell me."

The doorbell rang.

"I'll go," Zenobia said, running into the hall.

Annie was standing on the doorstep, surrounded by black plastic sacks.

"It's the jumble," she explained, "and my dad's gone home. Can I come in?"

Zenobia was staring at the bulging bags. "What's in them?"

"I don't know," Annie said. "My dad's been collecting them from lots of people."

"Can we look?" Zenobia asked.

Mum came to see what they were doing. "Hallo, Annie," she said. "My goodness — what a lot of jumble! It'll take ages to sort all that out." She picked up two of the bags and dragged them into the hall. Annie and

Zenobia pushed and pulled another one behind her but, just as they got into the kitchen, it split open and a tumble of old jumpers, tights, shoes, beads, curtains and hats spilt on to the floor.

"Oh dear," said Zenobia, looking at the mess.

Annie sat down in the middle of it and picked up a string of beads.

"Can we play Mummies and Daddies? We could dress up."

Mum plonked down her two bags of jumble and looked at Annie and Zenobia. "Wouldn't you like to go and play in Zenobia's room?" she suggested.

Annie shook her head. "We want to play Mummies and Daddies," she said, "don't we, Zenobia?"

Zenobia was trying on a large green velvet hat. "All right," she said.

Mum sighed. "Well — you can play with this pile of bits and pieces. But you must promise not to get in the way while I sort the other things."

Zenobia nodded, her hat flopping up and down. Annie was too busy wrapping herself up in a piece of white net to answer. She put on another string of beads and one pink high-heeled shoe.

"I'm a princess-mummy," she said. "You can be the daddy, Zenobia."

"I don't want to be a daddy," Zenobia said, pulling off her hat. Annie pounced on it and put it on.

"You've got to be the daddy, 'cause I'm the mummy. And we need a baby."

Zenobia stirred a bundle of tights with her foot.

"Oh!" Annie hurled herself on the floor and began throwing the tights in all directions.

"Look!" she squeaked, "look!"

Zenobia looked. Annie was cuddling a doll — a doll with big blue eyes and a happy smile.

"Oh — that's my doll." Zenobia put out a hand for Dollie May.

"She's not! She's not! She was in the things. I found her — she's mine!" Annie clutched Dollie May closely to her chest.

"But she's my Dollie May," said Zenobia crossly.

"No!" Annie shouted. "I *found* her! She's my baby — I can't be a proper mummy if I don't have a baby!" Tears rolled down her face.

"But she's mine!" Zenobia was beginning to cry as well. She tried to pull Dollie May away from Annie, but Annie held on tightly and screamed and screamed.

Mum came hurrying in from the hall. "Whatever is the matter?" she asked.

Annie held on tightly and
screamed and screamed.

"Zenobia, what *are* you doing?"

Zenobia flung herself at Mum. "Annie's trying to take Dollie May away from me!"

Mum sat down on the floor between Zenobia and Annie and put an arm round them both. Annie was sobbing loud hiccuppy sobs and hugging Dollie May, and Zenobia was snuffling loudly.

"It really is Zenobia's doll, Annie love," Mum said. "She must have got muddled up with the jumble — but I've just found a bag of toys. Maybe we could find you another doll." Annie went on crying.

"I only want this doll," she sobbed. "She smiles at me and she's the bestest baby ever."

"Let's just have a little look at the other toys," Mum said. She held out a hand to Zenobia. "Could Annie play with Dollie May just for now? And we'll fetch the bag in for her to see."

14

Zenobia sniffed, and glared at Annie. "But she *is* mine," she said as she got up. Annie stayed on the floor, rocking Dollie May to and fro.

Mum and Zenobia pulled in another plastic sack. Together they tipped it on to the floor, and old paintboxes, torn books, squashy balls and tangled-up skipping ropes fell out. There were two dolls with no hair, some pieces of train set and lots of bits of jigsaw puzzles.

"What about one of these, Annie?" Mum said, holding up one of the dolls.

Annie just sniffed miserably and shook her head.

Zenobia scrabbled about in the bottom of the bag, and pulled out some more books.

"Oh!" Zenobia sounded surprised. "I've found something else." She pulled out a long piece of string. The string was attached to a

"It's a mouse," Zenobia said,
stroking his tummy very gently.

soft furry bottom. She pulled again. A furry body with a big head, tattered pink ears and button eyes plopped on to the floor.

"It's a mouse," Zenobia said, stroking his tummy very gently.

"Isn't it a bear?" Mum asked.

"No. He's got a tail." Zenobia sat down and rested her chin on top of the mouse's head. It felt very comfortable.

"Look, Annie," Mum said, "wouldn't you like this mouse? Then you could give Zenobia back her doll."

"I only want the doll," Annie said in a wobbly voice. "I *need* the doll."

"I think I'll get us a drink and a biscuit," Mum said. "Will you come and help me?" She went to the kitchen cupboard, and Annie trailed after her holding Dollie May in her arms.

Zenobia didn't get up. She looked at the

mouse, and the mouse looked back at her. He wasn't smiling, but his eyes were very bright.

"Hallo, Mouse," Zenobia said quietly. Mouse's whiskers twitched.

"Mouse?"

Mouse closed one eye and opened it again. Zenobia stared at him.

"Oh, Mouse . . . dear Mouse, did you *hear* me?"

"I'm not deaf," Mouse said.

Zenobia gazed at him. She didn't hear Mum and Annie coming back.

"Here you are." Annie was standing beside Zenobia, holding out Dollie May. "Here's your doll." She rubbed her eyes.

Zenobia looked at Dollie May. Dollie May was still smiling, and her blue eyes were staring at the ceiling. Zenobia looked down at Mouse. His button eyes were shining. Zenobia took a deep breath.

"Annie can keep Dollie May," she said. "She can keep her for ever and ever." She looked at Mum. "And can I keep Mouse instead?"

"Of course you can," Mum said.

Annie rushed at Zenobia and hugged her. "I *love* you," she shouted.

Zenobia smiled and squeezed Mouse.

At the end of the day, Zenobia wriggled down in her bed. She yawned, and tucked Mouse under her arm.

"I had a dream last night," she said. "Shall I tell you?"

"Go on," said Mouse.

"It was a very noisy one," Zenobia said.

"Ah," said Mouse.

"If it comes again," Zenobia said thoughtfully, "you'll be here, won't you?"

"That's right," said Mouse.

"Do you think Dollie May is all right?"
Zenobia asked sleepily.

There was a silence.

"Do you think Dollie May is all right?" Zenobia asked sleepily.

"Yes," said Mouse firmly. "Quite all right."

"I expect she's still smiling," said Zenobia.

"I expect she is," said Mouse. "Tell me about your dream."

Zenobia snuggled down a little deeper. "Oh!" she said.

"What?" said Mouse.

"I've forgotten it."

"Ah," said Mouse. "Good night."

"What are you doing?" asked Mouse.
"Packing, of course," said Zenobia.

THE
HOT-WATER
BOTTLE

Zenobia pulled her suitcase out from under the bed.

"What are you doing?" asked Mouse.

"Packing, of course," said Zenobia.

Mouse scratched his ear. "Why?"

"Because we're going out with Gran and Grandpa. I told you."

Mouse scratched the other ear. "But we're only going out for tea."

"I might *need* things," said Zenobia, opening the case and putting three pairs of socks and her bedroom slippers inside.

"We'll be home by bedtime," Mouse said.

Zenobia packed a skirt, a book and her hot-water bottle. "Grandpa's car has creaks," she said. "It might stop and then we'd have to be in it all night, in the dark."

"Ah," said Mouse.

Zenobia looked round her room. She picked up a glove and another book and tucked them in the case with a scarf. Then she shut the lid and clicked the catches. "There we are."

"Pick it up," said Mouse.

Zenobia picked the case up and staggered. "It's very heavy."

"It's got lots of things in it," said Mouse.

"Yes." Zenobia put the case down. "P'raps I won't take it after all."

"Very wise," said Mouse.

"I'll just take the hot-water bottle."

They went downstairs.

Zenobia took her hot-water bottle into the kitchen, and filled it with cold water. "I'm not allowed hot water," she told Mouse.

"I know," said Mouse. "Mind you put the top on tightly."

"Are you ready, Zenobia?" Mum called. "Grandpa's here."

Zenobia rushed out of the kitchen. "Hurrah!" She flung her arms round Grandpa's neck.

"Ready?" he said, laughing.

"Nearly," said Zenobia. She puffed into the kitchen and snatched Mouse off the table and the hot-water bottle from the sink. "Where's my shopping bag?"

Mum unhooked the bag from behind the door. "Here you are."

Zenobia took the bag and slid the hot-water bottle inside. She hitched Mouse under her arm, gave Mum a kiss and ran down the steps to where Gran was waiting in the car.

Zenobia climbed into the back and settled

Mouse on the seat beside her.

"Hallo, duckie," said Gran. "Hallo, Mouse."

Grandpa started the car. There was a loud bang, and then a lot of little snorts. Zenobia giggled.

"What's your car saying today, Grandpa?"

"It says chinkelly chunk, chinkelly chunk," said Grandpa. "And it says it feels rather rattly today, so we'd better sing a song to help it along."

Gran and Grandpa and Zenobia began singing "Ten Green Bottles" very loudly.

The car gave a cheerful puff and a grunt and off they went.

It was a very good tea. Zenobia and Gran and Grandpa ate scones and jam and egg on toast and little chocolate cakes with cherries on the top. Mouse sat beside Zenobia on the shopping bag.

"It's rather cold," he said.

"Shhh," said Zenobia. She drank her milk shake up with a happy sloosh. "Can we sing on the way home, Grandpa?"

"I don't think the car will go if we don't, Zenobia," said Grandpa.

They sang "Old MacDonald had a Farm", and "This Old Man". It wasn't very loud singing because they were all very full, so when the car began to make a funny spitting noise, Grandpa heard it at once. He stopped at the side of the road.

"What's that smell?" asked Zenobia.

"I don't think my old friend is very well," said Grandpa. He got out, and went round to the front of the car. He opened up the bonnet, and the smell got stronger.

"I knew I ought to bring my bedroom slippers," Zenobia said.

"Bedroom slippers?" asked Gran.

Zenobia pulled her hot-water bottle
out of the shopping bag.

"For when we're here all night. I've got my hot-water bottle."

"Huh," said Mouse quietly. "Hot-water bottle!"

Grandpa came round to the car window.

"We will be here all night, won't we?" asked Zenobia.

Grandpa laughed.

"No – it's run out of water. All it needs is a drink."

Mouse coughed. Zenobia looked at him. He was sitting on the shopping bag on the floor of the car.

"Oh!" said Zenobia. "Grandpa! I know! I know! I've got some water!"

Grandpa was very surprised. He was even more surprised when Zenobia pulled her hot-water bottle out of the shopping bag.

"Well, well – pickle my whiskers! Who's a clever girl?"

Zenobia felt very pleased. Mouse coughed again, but Zenobia took no notice. She handed the hot-water bottle to Grandpa.

"Zenobia," said Grandpa, "it's empty."

Mouse sneezed.

Zenobia peered at the floor of the car. Mouse was sitting in a pool of water. "Oh dear," she said.

"Never mind," said Grandpa, "it's still just what we need." He walked across the road to a shop, and asked if he could fill up the hot-water bottle with cold water. When he came back the water trickled and bubbled and gurgled into the engine, and it started with no spitting noises at all.

"Shall we sing?" said Zenobia.

"Yes," said Gran, "let's sing three cheers for Zenobia, who saved the day!"

They reached Zenobia's house safely.

"Did you have a lovely time?" asked Mum.

"Yes!" said Zenobia. "And my hot-water bottle saved the day!"

Mouse sneezed.

"Huh," he said.

"Didn't you think it was a lovely outing?" Zenobia said.

"No," said Mouse.

"You are rather wet," said Zenobia, squeezing him.

"I told you to put the top on tightly," said Mouse.

"Well," said Zenobia, "it was quite tight."

Mouse sneezed again.

"Huh," he said.

Zenobia carried Mouse downstairs.
The house was very, very quiet.

ZENOBIA
MAKES A
SANDWICH

"Come on, Mouse," said Zenobia. "It's time for school."

"It's too early," said Mouse.

Zenobia was flinging on socks and pants and a back-to-front jumper. "We'll go downstairs," she said. "We'll surprise everybody."

"We certainly will," said Mouse. "They're all asleep."

Zenobia sneezed. "Shh," she said, "don't wake them up!"

Zenobia carried Mouse downstairs. The house was very, very quiet.

They went into the kitchen. PPPOP! Zenobia pulled the blind up. Mouse fell off the table.

Zenobia was looking in the fridge.

"Mouse — do you know what?"

"No," said Mouse from under the table.

"I'm going to make my own packed lunch."

Mouse sat up. "But your mum always makes it."

"I'm going to do it myself today." Zenobia went on peering in the fridge. "I'll have cheese and yogurt and an egg and a sausage and cucumber." She took out what she wanted and carried it to the table. The egg rolled off and fell on the floor with a wet plop.

"No egg," said Mouse.

Zenobia didn't answer. She was pulling a stool over to the shelves so that she could climb up and reach the bread.

"No!" Mouse squeaked fiercely. "You're not allowed to use the bread-knife!"

"I *know*," said Zenobia. She thought hard.

Then she took an ordinary knife from the drawer and sawed away at the loaf of bread.

"Oh dear," said Mouse.

"Look!" Zenobia said proudly. She held up her piece of bread.

"Isn't it rather thick?" Mouse asked.

"I like it like that," said Zenobia. She opened the tub of margarine and spread one side of the bread. Then she spread the other side and the edges as well.

"Oh dear," said Mouse.

"I like it like that," said Zenobia. Very carefully, she cut up pieces of cheese and cucumber and stuck them on the margarine. "It's an inside-out sandwich," she said.

"It's certainly different," said Mouse.

Zenobia looked at the uncooked sausage. It looked very pale and rubbery. "Can you eat them like that?" she asked.

"No," Mouse said firmly.

Zenobia left the sausage with the bread-crumbs, and took her lunch-box out of the cupboard. "It'll be the best packed lunch ever," she said proudly.

"Um," said Mouse.

Zenobia opened the fridge again. "I need a drink," she said. She took out a carton of milk, but as she carried it to the table, she slipped on the egg. "Whooops!" said Zenobia. She sucked her fingers. "Do you know what, Mouse?"

"No," said Mouse.

"I'm going to have orange juice instead. Claudia always has orange juice." Zenobia paddled through milk and egg on her way to the fridge. "My socks are wet," she said.

"So I see," said Mouse.

Zenobia took down the bottle of orange squash. It was nearly full, so it didn't really matter when a little spilt. Most of it went

*As Zenobia carried the carton to the
table, she slipped on the egg.*

into Zenobia's flask. She carefully added water and put the flask beside the lunch-box. "Sandwich and drink," Zenobia said. She put in the yogurt and a spoon.

"I think I'd like something else," she said thoughtfully.

"I think you've got enough," Mouse said.

"Adam always has *lots* of nice things," Zenobia said. She began hunting through the cupboards.

She found a pot of red sticky cherries, and chose four big ones.

She found currants and raisins, and took a handful of each.

She found two packets of jelly cubes, and pulled off three red cubes and three orange ones. Then she ate one from each packet.

"I haven't had any breakfast yet, you see," she told Mouse.

"Ah," said Mouse.

Zenobia put all the extras in her lunch-box. She topped it off with five chocolate biscuits and an ice-lolly from the freezer.

"It'll melt," said Mouse.

"It's a cold day," Zenobia said. She shut the lid of the lunch-box with a snap. "There! All ready! Won't Mum be pleased!"

"She'll be very surprised," said Mouse.

Zenobia ate another jelly cube.

"Even Emily has never had a lunch like mine," she said.

"I've just thought of something," Mouse said.

The kitchen door opened.

"Zenobia!" said Mum. "*Whatever* have you been doing?"

Zenobia smiled happily. "I'm all ready for school," she said. "I've made my lunch and I've had my breakfast. Oh — perhaps I ought to change my socks."

Under the table, Mouse nodded.
"That's what I thought," he said.

"But Zenobia," Mum said, "Zenobia —
it's Saturday today — there's no school!"

Under the table, Mouse nodded. "That's
what I thought," he said.

Quite a long time later, after a great deal of
mopping up, Zenobia said, "Do you know
what?"

"No?" said Mouse.

"We could have a picnic," said Zenobia.

"Good idea," said Mouse.

Zenobia fetched two cushions and settled
herself and Mouse in a corner of the kitchen
with the lunch-box.

"Actually," she said, "actually, I nearly
knew it was Saturday anyway."

"Ah," said Mouse.

Zenobia was very cross. She sat down on
the floor of the shop with a flump.

NEW
SHOES

Zenobia was very cross. She sat down on the floor of the shop with a flump, and stared at her knees.

"Ow!" said Mouse. Zenobia was sitting on his tail, and he didn't feel very comfortable.

"It's not fair," Zenobia said. "All Mum does is try on dresses, and I want to go and look at the shoe shop. She's tried on a spotty dress and a stripy one and a red one and a blue one and now she's trying on a frilly one. It's not fair."

"Ah," said Mouse.

"I don't expect I'll *ever* get any new shoes," Zenobia grumbled. "Mum says we're meeting Aunty Lou for a cup of something and they'll just talk and talk for ages and ages."

Mouse sighed. His tail was very flat and it didn't look as if Mum was going to make up her mind just yet. She was putting the frilly dress back on the rail and looking at a pink one.

"I hate pink," Zenobia said, glaring at Mum.

Mum picked the pink dress off the rail, and held it against herself.

"It's too little." Zenobia went on glaring.

Mum inspected her reflection in the long shop-mirror. "You're quite right," she said. "Did you like the blue one?"

"No," Zenobia said grumpily. "I didn't like any of them. I want some new shoes."

"I won't be a minute." Mum put the pink dress back.

"You've been lots and lots of minutes already. When can we buy my shoes?"

"We didn't come out shopping to buy you shoes, Zenobia," Mum said. "We came to look at dresses and meet Aunty Lou. Besides, even if we *were* looking at shoes I wouldn't buy them for a horrid, cross girl — only cheerful girls, who wait patiently, get new shoes."

Zenobia made a growly noise and pulled Mouse's ears.

"Ouch!" Mouse said, indignantly. "What did I do?"

Zenobia and Mum met Aunty Lou at the little café on the corner of the road. Mum was very pleased to see Aunty Lou and she showed her the new blue dress. Zenobia didn't say anything.

"It's very pretty," said Aunty Lou. "Do you like it, Zenobia?"

Zenobia opened her mouth to say that she didn't like it one little bit, and then she remembered what Mum had said about not buying shoes for cross girls.

"It's quite nice," she said. She made her face twist into a smile. "It's just the right size."

Aunty Lou laughed. "I'm glad of that," she said. "And what have you bought, Zenobia?"

Zenobia wriggled. "Nothing yet."

"Would you like a strawberry ice-cream?" Aunty Lou was reading the menu.

Zenobia said that she would, very much. Then she looked at Mum and added, "Thank you very much, Aunty Lou."

"You're very polite today, Zenobia," Aunty Lou said. "Do you want a drink as well?"

Zenobia smiled again. It felt a more real smile this time. "Yes, please. Thank you."

Aunty Lou ordered one ice-cream, one lemonade and two cups of coffee. Then she and Mum began to talk, just as Zenobia had

"It's quite nice," Zenobia said.
"It's just the right size."

expected. Aunty Lou talked about blue hats, and Mum talked about red hats. They both talked about dresses and shoes. Then they pulled Mum's new dress out of its bag, and they talked about that. Zenobia sat and ate her ice-cream very slowly, and tried to see how long she could make it last.

Mum asked Aunty Lou if she remembered Mrs somebody's hat. Aunty Lou gave a little scream, and they talked some more. Zenobia licked the last dribble of ice-cream off her spoon, and put it down. She had a sip of lemonade, and rearranged Mouse on the chair beside her.

Aunty Lou asked Mum if she remembered a Mrs somebody else's shoes. It was Mum's turn to give a little scream. Aunty Lou moved her chair closer to Mum's and they went on talking in whispery voices. Zenobia spooned some lemonade out of her glass and into her mouth. Then she licked her finger and dipped it in the sugar. She gave Mum a quick sideways glance to see if she had noticed, but Mum was still talking and waving her hands about. Zenobia sucked her finger and then had another spoonful of lemonade. She started to sigh, but rememberd that she was trying not to be cross half-way through and swallowed the sigh down. Something happened to it when it met the lemonade — and Zenobia began to hiccup loudly.

Mum stopped talking. "Whatever's the matter? Was your lemonade too fizzy?"

Zenobia shook her head, and another loud hiccup squeezed out.

"Oh!" she gasped. "I didn't mean it." She hugged Mouse tightly to her in order to stop the next hiccup, but it seemed to make it worse.

"Have a drink of water," Aunty Lou

*Most of the water went
all over Mouse.*

suggested. She passed Zenobia a glass and poured some water into it, but when Zenobia drank it, the water and the hiccup got muddled up and most of the water went all over Mouse.

"Oh, *Zenobia*!" Mum said. "What a mess!" She didn't sound very pleased.

Zenobia snatched at a paper napkin just as Aunty Lou leant forward to look at the mess, and their heads crashed together.

"OH!"

"OW!"

"Oh dear," said Mum.

But Aunty Lou began to laugh. "Did you see stars, Zenobia?"

Zenobia shook her head, and then looked surprised. "Oh!" she said. "Listen!"

Mum and Aunty Lou stared at her.

"My hiccups have stopped," she said.

"There you are," Aunty Lou said. "I knew

the water would make you better." She rubbed her head. "Or perhaps it was the bump on the head! Now — you've been a very patient girl — what are we going to do?"

Zenobia jumped up from her chair in excitement. "Have I really?" she asked.

"What?" Aunty Lou was puzzled.

"Have I really been a patient girl?"

"You really have," Aunty Lou said firmly. Zenobia hopped up and down.

"Can we go and get my shoes now?" She tugged at Mum's arm. "You said we could — you *said* you'd buy me my shoes. You said cheerful girls who wait patiently get new shoes, and Aunty Lou said I was *very* patient — so now I can have my shoes?"

Mum sighed, and picked up her bag. "I give in. You do need new ones." She took Zenobia's hand. Aunty Lou tucked Mouse under her arm and took Zenobia's other hand. "Ready?" she asked.

"Let's go," Mum said, smiling.

"Hurrah for Zenobia," said Mouse, very quietly.

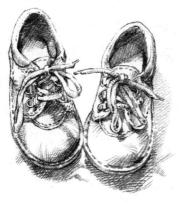

Zenobia looked at her rabbit-clock
beside her bed.

WILD
LIFE

It was early in the morning. The sun was floating in little golden sparkles through the gap in the curtains and shining on Zenobia's face. Zenobia opened her eyes and sneezed.

"Oooof," she said, and sat up in bed.

"Um," said Mouse, from under the duvet.

Zenobia looked at the sunshine, and she looked at her rabbit-clock beside her bed. There was something wrong, and she couldn't think what it was. "Mouse," she said, "why isn't today all right?"

Mouse yawned. "Isn't it?"

"No. My tummy feels funny but I don't feel sick."

"What sort of funny?"

Zenobia thought about it.

"It feels as if something's got in there by mistake, and I don't much like it."

Mouse scratched his ears. "Maybe you should call Mum."

Zenobia shook her head. "It isn't poorly," she said. "It's just funny. Like when I go to see the dentist."

"Ah." Mouse stopped scratching and sat up. "Are you going to the dentist today?"

"No. Only school."

"Oh," Mouse said.

Mum came into Zenobia's room, and drew back the curtains. "It's a lovely day," she said. "It couldn't be better for an outing. Hop out of bed and whizz downstairs."

Zenobia sat up in bed and stared at Mum. Her eyes grew large and anxious. "Outing?" she squeaked.

"You can't have forgotten," Mum said.

"It's today you're all going out for the day."

"I think my tummy remembered," Zenobia said, her voice still squeaky.

Mum looked at Zenobia. "Are you feeling poorly?"

Zenobia swallowed, and felt a lump in her throat. "My throat hurts," she said.

Mum put her hand on Zenobia's forehead to see if it was hot. Then she peered inside her mouth.

"I can't see anything," Mum said. "Does it hurt a lot?"

"It feels all lumpy," Zenobia said. "And my tummy feels even worse."

Mum sat on the edge of the bed and looked at Zenobia. "You'd better stay in bed for a little while longer. I'll fetch you a drink."

Zenobia felt much better at once. "Can I have hot chocolate?" she asked.

"I expect so." Mum said, as she went out.

Zenobia sighed and curled up in bed.

"I think my throat really does hurt a lot," she told Mouse.

"Why?" Mouse asked.

"It isn't why," Zenobia said. "Throats just do or don't hurt."

"Ah," said Mouse.

Mum came back carrying a tray. There was a plate of bread and butter, a banana, an apple and Zenobia's special mug full of hot chocolate.

"See if you can eat a little," Mum said as she put the tray on the bedside table.

Zenobia swallowed again. The lump was smaller. "I might eat a little bit," she said.

"Good." Mum helped Zenobia to sit up, and patted her. "I'll be back in a minute."

Zenobia sipped the chocolate, and nibbled a piece of bread and butter. Then she ate the banana. Then she ate the apple. And then

Mum helped Zenobia to sit up,
and patted her.

she ate some more of the bread and butter.

"Feeling better?" Mouse asked.

"Shh," said Zenobia. She finished her chocolate with a slurp, and then ate the last piece of bread and butter. "That was nice," she said.

"How's your tummy?"

Zenobia gave Mouse a cross look. "It still feels different."

"It probably feels full," Mouse said.

Zenobia pushed Mouse under the duvet.

Dad put his head round the door. "Not feeling well, chicken?" he asked.

"Not very," Zenobia said sadly. Then she sat up straighter. "Could I have some more bread and butter?"

Dad laughed and took the plate. "That sounds hopeful."

"And some more hot chocolate?"

"Dear, dear." Dad picked up the banana

skin and the apple core. "Sure there's nothing else you'd like?"

"Are there any spotty biscuits?"

Dad piled the bits on to the tray. "Hot chocolate, biscuits and bread and butter. My word, chicken, you'll be too fat to go on your outing."

Zenobia opened her mouth but didn't say anything. Dad went off with the tray.

Mouse made a squeaky noise from under the bedclothes.

"What is it?" Zenobia asked, as she pulled him out.

"I've been wondering," Mouse said.

"Well?" Zenobia asked.

"Why don't you want to go on the class outing?"

Zenobia flopped back on to her pillow. She didn't look at Mouse, but picked at the edge of the duvet with her finger.

"There's going to be wild things," she said in a wobbly voice.

"What?"

Zenobia picked Mouse up and buried her nose in him. She began to cry. "I don't want to see wild things," she snuffled, "they might eat me."

"There can't be any wild things," Mouse said in a smothered voice.

"There are — Mrs Graham said so," Zenobia sobbed. "We're going on a walk to find wild things and bring them back into our classroom so they'll be there for ever and ever." She let out a loud wail.

Mum and Dad hurried in.

"Whatever's the matter, lovey?" Mum asked. "Is your throat worse?"

Zenobia flung herself on Mum's chest. "Don't make me go," she howled, "I don't want to go."

Zenobia flung herself
on Mum's chest.

Dad said, "Here, blow your nose, my poor
little dumpling – and I'll explain."

Dad sat down on the bed beside Zenobia. "What's all this about?"

"It's the wild things," Zenobia said in a wet and sniffly voice. She gave a loud sob. "I don't want to collect any wild animals or *anything*."

Mum patted Zenobia's back, and Dad patted her knee.

"There won't be anything scary," Dad said. "Mrs Graham always looks after you — and everyone else in the class."

"But she *said*," Zenobia insisted. "She said we'd go and find wild lifes and bring them back. We're going to have little bottles to put them in — but they might get out!"

Dad pulled a big red hanky out of his pocket. "Here, blow your nose, my poor little dumpling — and I'll explain."

Zenobia blew her nose very hard and sat up on Mum's knee.

"What's a buttercup?" Dad asked.

Zenobia stared at him. "A flower," she said.

"And a daisy?"

Zenobia forgot to snuffle. She smiled. "Another flower. Everybody knows that."

"Well," Dad said, "some people call them wild flowers — that means they grow without our help. But they don't bite, do they?"

Zenobia giggled. "Flowers don't bite, silly Dad."

"Right. Well, people call worms, tadpoles, spiders and flies wild life — all the little things that you find in the garden and in the park. That's what Mrs Graham means."

"I don't like spiders much," Zenobia said.

"But they don't eat you," Mum said. "And they can't even tickle you if they're safe in a bottle."

Zenobia was very quiet for a moment.

Then she looked up.

"Can I have more bread and butter and hot chocolate when I'm dressed?"

Zenobia was ready to go on the outing. She had on her jeans and her anorak, and her packed lunch was in a shoulder bag.

"I'll take you in the car," Dad said. "Just in case a wild thing attacks you in the high street."

Zenobia made a face at him. "I won't be a minute." She flew up the stairs to her room, and came back with Mouse under her arm.

"It's just in case," she said. She looked at Dad out of the corner of her eye. "I mean, even if the wild lifes are very little, I might need a wild Mouse to look after me."

Dad laughed, and went out to the car. Zenobia followed with Mouse.

"Grrrr," said Mouse.

"Lions aren't pink," said Mouse.
"Mine are," Zenobia said.

ZENOBIA
HAS A
BATH

"I don't like baths," Zenobia said. "I'll have one tomorrow instead."

She went on colouring her picture. "I'm going to draw some wild lions."

"That's clever," said Mouse.

"Zenobia! Are you getting undressed?" Mum called. "Your bath's ready."

Zenobia didn't move. Mouse looked over her shoulder.

"Lions aren't pink."

"Mine are," Zenobia said.

"So are your fingers," said Mouse. "And you've got blue smudges on your nose."

Zenobia rubbed at her nose, and left a pink streak beside the blue smudge. Mouse began to laugh, and Zenobia giggled. "Do I look like a rainbow?" she asked.

"Almost," said Mouse, "but rainbows have more colours."

Zenobia giggled again. "I'm going to look in the mirror."

"But you haven't got a mirror," Mouse said.

"I'll look in the bathroom. But I'm not having a bath." Zenobia got up, and she and Mouse went upstairs.

The bathroom was very steamy. Zenobia climbed on a stool, but the mirror was clouded over. "I can't see," she complained.

"Wipe it," Mouse said.

Zenobia climbed down and fetched her flannel. After she had wiped the mirror, she peered at her face. "I look funny," she said.

"What sort of funny?" asked Mouse.

"Funny funny," said Zenobia. "I'm going

to be a proper rainbow." She dropped her flannel on the floor and jumped off the stool.

"Um," said Mouse.

"And I'm going to finish my picture," Zenobia said as she stumped out of the bathroom and went downstairs again.

"Zenobia! Aren't you undressed yet?" Mum called.

"Can't I finish my picture?"

"Two minutes, or I'll be very cross."

"Actually," Zenobia shouted, "I don't think I want a bath."

"Two minutes."

Mouse watched Zenobia draw a big yellow sun above the pink lions.

"That's pretty," he said.

Zenobia laughed. "Look." She drew a sun on each of her cheeks.

"Ooooh," said Mouse.

Zenobia drew several wiggly green stripes on her picture, and several more on her chin.

"Those are trees," she said. "Do I look like a real rainbow now?"

"I'm not quite sure," said Mouse. "It's certainly different."

Zenobia added some orange dots to her picture and some more to her nose.

"Um." Mouse smoothed his whiskers.

"I had to do some flowers on the trees," Zenobia explained. "Shall we go and look now?"

The stool was still in front of the mirror in the bathroom. Zenobia climbed back up, and stared at her face.

"It's not *very* much like a rainbow," said Mouse carefully.

"Oh."

"What do you think?" asked Mouse.

"It's horrid," said Zenobia. "I want to

Zenobia climbed back up,
and stared at her face.

wash it off." She got down, and began pulling off her clothes. "It looks all messy — it's not a bit like a rainbow."

"Oh dear," said Mouse.

Zenobia peeled off her socks, and jumped into the bath.

"Oh! It's cold!"

She scrambled out again, spattering the floor with water. "I don't like cold baths," she said.

Mouse shook the water off his whiskers. "Nor do I," he said.

"But I need to wash my face." Zenobia dipped Mum's sponge in the bath, and rubbed it hard with soap. Then she began to scrub her face. The sponge turned a soapy blue and pink and green.

"Ow! Ow! Ow!" Zenobia shrieked, "My eyes hurt! Ow!" She began to cry very loudly.

Mum came hurrying into the bathroom. "Whatever's going on?"

Zenobia was rubbing at her eyes with a towel. Both the towel and her face were all smudgy and wet with crying.

"Oh, Zenobia!" said Mum. She wrapped Zenobia up in a clean towel, and poured some of her very special face-cream on to a handful of cotton wool. Then she wiped Zenobia's face very carefully.

"No! No!" Zenobia wriggled and squirmed. "I don't like it!"

"Keep still just a little longer, lovey," said Mum. "I've nearly finished."

Zenobia kept her eyes shut tight. "Has it all gone?" she asked anxiously.

"Nearly," said Mum. "If you hop in the bath and have a good wash it will all disappear."

"The water's cold," Zenobia said.

75

Mouse leant forward to look at Zenobia.
"You still have orange flowers on your nose."

"I'll put in some more hot." Mum turned on the tap, and swished the water round. "There you are. Jump in, and I'll come and dry you in five minutes."

"Is my face better now?" Zenobia lay back in the bath with a flannel on her tummy.

"Lots better," Mouse said.

"Is it quite clean?"

Mouse was sitting on the towel-rail. He leant forward to look at Zenobia. "You still have orange flowers on your nose."

Zenobia swooshed the water up and down, and splashed her face. "Oooof! Now it's all gone!"

"Very nearly," said Mouse.

There was a tremendous swirling and sploshing, and Zenobia climbed out of the bath in a flurry of drips and drops.

"Where are you going?" asked Mouse.

"I'm looking for myself." Zenobia got on to the stool, and peered in the mirror. She rubbed furiously at her nose. "There!" she said happily. "It's all gone." She flapped her flannel at Mouse.

There was a small splash, and a loud squeak.

"Oh no!" Zenobia jumped off the stool, and pulled Mouse out of the bath. He was coughing and spluttering, and Zenobia put him on the bath-rack to drip.

"Poor Mouse," she said, and got back into the bath.

Mum came up to help Zenobia get dry. She looked at the wet and dripping Mouse.

"Oh dear," she said. "I'd better take Mouse downstairs and put him on a radiator. I don't think he likes baths."

"I do," said Zenobia, swilling water round

her toes. "I love baths. Can I stay in for hours and hours?"

"Well — just a moment or two," Mum said.

"Two minutes?"

"All right," said Mum.

"Actually," Zenobia said thoughtfully, "I think I'll have another bath tomorrow."

"Atchoooo!" said Mouse.